The

MASTERS

Published by Creative Education, Inc.

123 South Broad Street, Mankato, MN 56001

Designed by Rita Marshall with the help of Thomas Lawton

Cover illustration by Rob Day, Lance Hidy Associates

Copyright © 1993 by Creative Education, Inc.

All rights reserved. No part of this book may be reproduced

in any form without written permission from the publisher.

Photography by Allsport, Duomo, Focus on Sports,

FPG International, Sportschrome, Wide World Photos

Printed in the United States

Library of Congress Cataloging-in-Publication Data

Deegan, Paul J., 1937–

The Masters / Paul Deegan.

p.   cm.—(Great moments in sports)

Summary: Presents highlights from the professional golf

tournament held each April in Augusta, Georgia.

ISBN 0-88682-535-0

1. Masters Golf Tournament, Augusta, Ga.—History—

Juvenile literature.   [1. Masters Golf Tournament—

History.   2. Golf—Tournaments—History.]   I. Title.

II. Series.

GV970.D44   1992

796.352'66—dc20

92-3724

CIP

AC

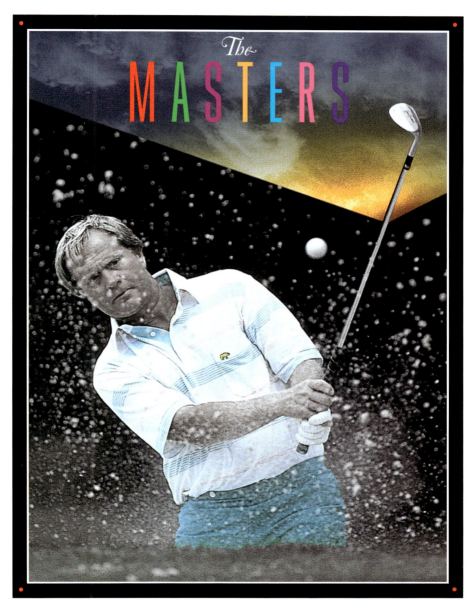

PAUL DEEGAN

CREATIVE EDUCATION INC.

On this spring day in 1990, Englishman Nick Faldo knew he had a chance to make Masters Tournament history. He had won the tournament in 1989. If he could win this year's tournament, he would become only the second player to win two straight Masters. Jack Nicklaus had accomplished this feat in 1965 and 1966. Maybe now it was Faldo's turn.

Duplicating his 1989 victory would hardly be easy, however. After three rounds, he was three strokes off the pace set by Raymond Floyd. And the record-holder himself, fifty-year-old Jack Nicklaus, was only two strokes behind Faldo. But despite the pressure, Nick Faldo kept a positive attitude. His 1989 victory had come in a sudden-death play-off. "I kept on thinking that maybe history was going to repeat itself," he said.

Nick Faldo.

Early Sunday afternoon, on the final day of the tournament, Faldo's chances seemed to fade. Raymond Floyd had played twelve of the eighteen holes and his lead was now four strokes. Floyd, who had won the Masters fourteen years ago, was in a commanding position to win the fifty-fourth Masters. "After the twelfth hole, I didn't think I could lose," Floyd said.

Raymond Floyd won the Masters in 1976.

Then Faldo played the twelfth hole. He dropped a fifteen-foot birdie putt from the fringe of the green. He continued with birdies on the par-5 thirteenth and fifteenth holes. And at hole sixteen he stroked a twenty-foot birdie putt. Now he trailed Floyd by only one stroke.

Would Faldo join Nicklaus as the only player to win back-to-back Masters Tournaments?

BOBBY JONES'S DREAM

The Masters Tournament is one of the best-known professional golf tournaments. Held each April in Augusta, Georgia, the Masters serves as a magnet to the golfing world. Exciting finishes and play-offs thrill those fans fortunate enough to be present; millions more watch the Masters' great moments on television. For the golfers themselves, slipping into the winner's traditional green sports jacket, held by the previous year's winner, is a career highlight. Winning the Masters brings a player instant recognition and marks him as special for the rest of his life.

The Masters is so special, in fact, that a ticket to the tournament may be the hardest ticket to get in sports. Daily tickets have not been available since 1967. A waiting list of thousands was closed in 1978.

The Masters Tournament is a springtime tradition.

The tournament was developed in the 1930s under the guidance of Bobby Jones, an important figure in U.S. golf history. In 1926 Jones became the first player to win the U.S. Open and the British Open in the same season. In 1930 he became the first player to win the "Grand Slam" of golf—winning four major tournaments in the same year. During the eight years he played tournament golf, 1923 to 1930, he won thirteen of the twenty-one major championships in which he competed. Although Bobby Jones was only five foot eight, he could power a golf ball with his marvelous, fluid swing. In 1929 one writer referred to Jones as "simply the most stupendous golfer the game has ever known."

Bobby Jones.

Bernhard Langer displays a smooth swing in the 1988 Masters.

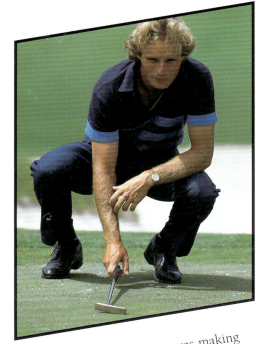

At the time Bobby Jones was making his mark on the sport, golf was mainly popular in Great Britain, where it had been played for over four centuries. But the dynamic playing of Bobby Jones and others helped the game take hold in the United States. It seems appropriate that Jones would also be responsible for one of today's best-loved tournaments.

Langer won the Masters Tournament in 1985.

In 1930 Jones retired from competitive golf and began pursuing a new dream—developing the ideal golf course. Land for the course was purchased in 1931 in Augusta, Georgia, some 150 miles east of Atlanta. The site was chosen in part for its mild climate, allowing year-round play. With British doctor Alister Mackenzie, Jones set about designing the Augusta National Golf Club.

Severiano Ballesteros, champion of the Masters in 1980 and 1983.

Soon another man, Clifford Roberts, joined the pair. Roberts was a New York stockbroker who came to Augusta for wintertime golf. It was his suggestion that the Augusta National Golf Club start its own tournament. He wanted to call it the Masters Tournament, but Bobby Jones thought the name was overblown. The official title in the early years was the Augusta National Invitation Tournament. The Masters name caught on early, however, and became the tournament's title in 1939.

On March 22, 1934, Bobby Jones came out of retirement to smack a drive 270 yards down the middle of the fairway on the first hole of the Augusta National Golf Course. A great tradition had begun.

The historic clubhouse.

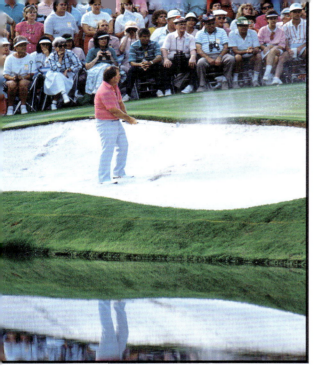

From the beginning, the Masters was a four-day tournament, unlike other major golf tournaments in the 1930s, which were three days and ended with thirty-six holes on a Saturday. The Masters finished on a Sunday with a fourth eighteen-hole round. Today, particularly because of the large television audience on Sundays, this is the format for almost all tournaments.

Clifford Roberts continued to have a great influence on the tournament. He served as tournament chair for the first Masters and ran the event with an iron hand until he died in 1977 at the age of eighty-three. Jones died in 1971, after enduring a crippling disease for many years.

Craig Stadler, winner of the 1982 Masters Tournament, works his way out of a sand trap.

Each April in the city of Augusta, however, their legacy continues.

A DOUBLE EAGLE

Gene Sarazen stood on the fifteenth tee during the final scheduled round of the 1935 Masters. Sarazen was glum. He had

captured many major titles in his career. But now, with four holes to play, he was three strokes down to Craig Wood, who had already completed his round.

Tom Watson claimed the Masters title in 1977 and 1981.

Sarazen's chances of winning the second Masters Tournament were very slim, but he kept his cool. The fifteenth was a par-5 hole. "I've got to make up one of my strokes on this hole," Sarazen thought. He hit a solid shot off the tee. Then he decided to go for the water-fronted green on just his second shot. His playing partner, the legendary Walter Hagen, shook his head. Bobby Jones, the tournament's founder, waited with great interest by the green. Both men had to admire Sarazen's willingness to go for it.

Gene Sarazen.

Sarazen started to pull a 3-wood from his bag. Then he changed his mind and chose a 4-wood. He took his fairway shot and watched the ball sail toward the green. The ball struck the far bank of the water, jumped onto the putting surface, and continued rolling and rolling until, before Bobby Jones's eyes, it plopped into the cup.

Sarazen had a two—a double eagle! A double eagle (three under par for a hole) is even rarer than a hole in one, and almost unheard of in major competition. A combination of guts and luck had brought about one of the greatest moments in Masters play. Sarazen had caught Craig Wood with one shot!

Sarazen maintained his tie with Wood by parring the last three holes. The next day he whipped Wood by five strokes in a thirty-six-hole play-off to win the 1935 Masters.

Sarazen's spectacular shot helped popularize the Masters Tournament among top players and the general public. It received so much attention, in fact, that it came to be known as "the shot heard around the world."

Sandy Lyle dons the championship jacket in 1988.

PALMER'S RUN

It was the 1962 Masters Tournament. Arnold Palmer, the superstar credited with making golf a household word, was once again battling for a green coat in Augusta. "Mr. Golf" had already won two Masters titles. Now, on his final round of the 1962 tournament, he trailed another great player, South Africa's Gary Player, by two strokes with only nine holes to play.

Arnold Palmer.

A long putt on the 13th green.

Palmer wasn't feeling very confident. Earlier in the tournament he'd held a two-stroke lead and had thought he could break the Masters' seventy-two-hole record of 274 strokes. But now the record was no longer in reach. "You always think that you're smarter at the game," he said later. "But every now and then you realize you're not as smart as you thought you were."

Palmer was still very much in the game, however, and no one knew that better than Gary Player. "I have a very uncomfortable feeling when Arnold is behind me, breathing down my neck," Player admitted during the tournament. "I'd rather be a stroke behind him than a stroke ahead of him."

Gary Player.

As they approached the par-3 sixteenth hole, Palmer was still chasing Player. Palmer drove to near the green, then reached into his bag for a wedge. "There's not much time left for me to do something," he thought. "I've got to make something happen here." He hit his wedge, then stood watching as the ball went into the cup for a birdie. The margin was down to one stroke—but not for long.

Sam Snead plays in the 1984 tournament, thirty years after his last Masters victory.

On the next hole Palmer hit a great 8-iron shot to within twelve feet of the pin. Then he stroked a twelve-foot putt into the hole for a second straight birdie. He had finally caught Player. The two men finished regulation play in a three-way tie for the lead, joined by Dow Finsterwald.

The next day the trio began an eighteen-hole play-off. (The first sudden-death play-off at the Masters came in 1979.) After nine holes, Palmer again found himself trailing Player, this time by three strokes.

Palmer has said that one of the most important lessons of golf is learning how to live with trouble. "You've got to learn to get out of it," he explained. "You've got to make good things happen. You can't stand back and expect them [the other players] to roll over."

The leaders scoreboard.

Palmer put his philosophy into action. His magnificent game suddenly fell into place once again as he birdied five of the first seven holes on the back nine. This memorable Masters moment enabled him to play the final nine holes four under par, giving him a three-stroke win. This was the third of the four Masters tournaments he was to win during his career. Only Jack Nicklaus, with six titles, has more victories at the Masters.

NICKLAUS HANGS ON

Jack Nicklaus had just bogeyed the ninth hole at Augusta National. He had led the 1966 Masters Tournament several times; now he trailed. But the twenty-six-year-old golfer, who had won the tournament the previous year, stayed calm. "Right then I got a grip on myself," he explained later. "I hit some bad shots after that, but no dumb ones."

Jack Nicklaus has won more Masters Tournaments than any other golfer.

Jack Nicklaus, nicknamed "the Golden Bear."

One of those bad shots came off the tee on number fourteen. Nicklaus's tee shot went into the tree and rebounded back into the fairway. He was much farther from the green than he wanted to be. And he was now three strokes behind the leader, Gay Brewer. How could he get back into the match now?

Nicklaus soon answered that question. He nailed a 3-iron to within six feet of the pin. He dropped the putt for a birdie and shaved a stroke off Brewer's margin. A great fairway iron shot on the fifteenth hole gave him a second birdie. Now he trailed by one stroke. At that point, Gay Brewer helped Nicklaus out by missing a five-foot putt for a par on the final hole.

Nicklaus, along with Tommy Jacobs, tied Brewer at even par for the four rounds, forcing a play-off for the championship. "Sheer perseverance" was the only thing that had kept him in the running, Nicklaus said later. "I was proud of the way I managed to come back . . . when it looked as if I was definitely out of the tournament."

Gay Brewer.

Pages 20–21: The beautiful sixteenth hole at Augusta National.

Now the question became whether or not Nicklaus could defend his 1965 Masters victory. He told others, "I've blown this tournament three times. But I don't intend to blow it again."

Standing over his ball on the eleventh play-off hole the following day, Nicklaus faced a twenty-five-foot birdie putt. He

Lee Trevino at the 1989 Masters.

studied the putt and approached the ball. He stroked it. A few seconds later his caddie was leaping in the air. Nicklaus had made the putt. His birdie, later called "the key shot of the play-off," gave him a two-stroke lead. Seven holes later he finished a two-under-par round of seventy. His two-stroke lead held up and the victory was his. Nicklaus had won successive Masters championships, something no one else had ever done.

Three years earlier, the young superstar from Ohio had experienced another memorable moment at the Masters, winning the tournament for the first time and at twenty-three becoming the youngest winner in tournament history. That 1963 win made a profound impression on him. Although it was not as dramatic as his 1966 victory, he learned a valuable lesson from it that would stay with him the rest of his career.

The third round of the 1963 tournament was played in rainy weather, unusual for the Masters. Nicklaus was playing with tour veteran Mike Souchak, who was the leader going into the round. "When we came to the thirteenth hole, the entire fairway area seemed to be under water," Nicklaus recalled. All he could do, he decided, was to keep plodding on as best he could.

Augusta can be a difficult course, even for the pros.

Nicklaus and his caddie size up a putt.

When he got to the eighteenth hole and the leader board was visible, Nicklaus saw his name on top. "Suddenly I realized that simply by hanging in there, I was leading the Masters," he said.

This Masters moment stayed with Nicklaus as he took his place as the dominant golfer of the 1960s and 1970s. "Most golf tournaments are not so much won by playing well," he said, "as they are not lost when opportunity presents itself." This realization brought him a lot more first-place finishes, especially in the majors.

As an example of how difficult tournament golf can be, Nicklaus, whose six wins in the Masters is a record, missed the cut in 1967, the year following his back-to-back victories. He came back to Augusta to win the Masters again in 1972 and 1975, and again in 1986 when he was forty-six years old.

Ben Crenshaw, the 1984 Masters champion.

FALDO REIGNS

The fifty-third Masters was the site of another dramatic battle between the world's best golfers. Forty-nine-year-old Lee Trevino, who had won all the other Grand Slam tournaments twice but had never won the Masters; Spain's Severiano Ballesteros, twice a winner in Augusta; Ben Crenshaw, the 1984 Masters champion; and Greg Norman all made strong runs at the 1989 Masters title while playing through four days of cold and rain.

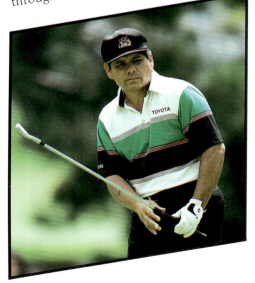

Lee Trevino.

"Sevvy" Ballesteros, champion golfer from Spain.

But when the final scheduled eighteen holes were completed on Sunday, none of the four was on top of the leader board. Instead, thirty-one-year-old Englishman Nick Faldo and the American Scott Hoch were tied for the lead and headed for the sudden-death play-off.

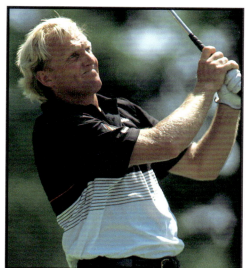

For Faldo it had been a long haul. Rain had driven him and thirteen other players off the course before they could finish Saturday's round; they had been forced to complete third-round play on Sunday morning. Faldo finished the round with seventy-seven strokes, and was definitely not happy. He was especially concerned about his putting.

Greg Norman.

"But then I thought 'you're only five shots back,' " he told reporters. "This is the hardest tournament in the world to win if you lead after three rounds." That reminder to himself made a big difference in his game. On Sunday afternoon Faldo played the first nine holes of the fourth and final round in thirty-two strokes. On the back nine he had four birdies on a course slowed by several days of rain. That gave him a seven-under-par round of sixty-five —and a tie for the lead. On the eighteenth hole, Scott Hoch missed a birdie putt by inches, one that would have earned him the championship.

The sudden-death play-off was on, and one of the most tense moments came on the first play-off hole. Faldo had bogeyed the par-4 tenth hole. Hoch faced another putt for the championship. This attempt for par was from only two feet. Every golfer knows the pressure of putting when something is at stake. And the pressure is there, even for a professional golfer, especially when facing a putt which will win— or lose—a major tournament.

Those watching could hardly believe it, however, when Hoch butchered the putt, stroking it four feet past the cup. "I just thought, well, he's opened the door for me," Faldo said. "Then it felt like destiny."

Minutes later the British golfer was facing a twenty-five-foot birdie putt on the second play-off hole. If he made it, he would win the Masters. In a great Masters moment, Faldo stroked it into the center of the cup and the championship was his.

Nick Faldo and his caddie at the 1990 British Open.

Scott Hoch chips one up the green.

Ian Woosnam, winner of the 1991 championship.

In 1987 Faldo had won the British Open by only a stroke, but he said his first Masters victory was more of a battle. "To come and to win in America, to be honest, is harder," he said.

A DRAMATIC FINISH

A year later there would be another dramatic finish on the Augusta National course, one more great moment in the history of the Masters Tournament.

Nick Faldo had fought back to within a stroke of tournament leader Raymond Floyd. He was seeking his second straight win, which would equal Jack Nicklaus's feat in 1965 and 1966. He got the break he needed when Floyd three-putted on the seventeenth hole. The bogey dropped Floyd into a tie with Faldo. The British golf star finished his round in sixty-nine, three under par, to tie Floyd for first place. It was Faldo's second two-man sudden-death Masters play-off in two years. The tension was tremendous, but Faldo felt confident. "It seemed like maybe it was going to happen," he said after the match.

Raymond Floyd.

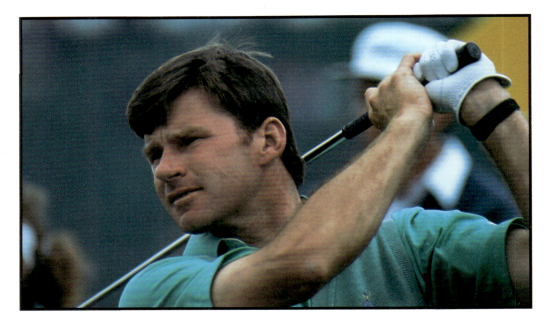

As had happened the previous year, Faldo's opponent had a potential winning putt on the first play-off hole, number ten. But Raymond Floyd's fifteen-footer was barely short, and now both players had par fours. On the second play-off hole, Floyd's second shot headed into a pond alongside the eleventh green. He had to take a drop. Given the opportunity to play safely, Faldo two-putted from eighteen feet for a par four and his second green coat in two straight years.

"Things turned out about the same as a year ago," Faldo said happily. "I've won three majors now, but this is the best."

To many pro golfers and their fans, that would also be a fair description of the Masters Tournament—"the best."

The champion.